COLLECT THE SET!

Boffin Boy and the Invaders from Space
978 184167 613 5

Boffin Boy and the Wizard of Edo
978 184167 614 2

Boffin Boy and the Monsters from the Deep
978 18 67 615 9

Boffin y and the Red Wolf
978 18 7 616 6

Boffin y and the Lost City
978 184 7 617 3

y and the Time Warriors
7 622 7

Boy and the Ice Caves of Pluto
7 626 5

y and the Quest for Wisdom
7 628 9

Bo y and the Deadly Swarm
978 7 625 8

Boff and the Rock Men
978 1 624 1

Boffin Boy and the Temples of Mars
978 184167 623 4

Boffin Boy and the Forest of the Ninja
978 184167 6

Boffin Boy and the Ice Caves of Pluto
by David Orme

Illustrated by Peter Richardson

Published by Ransom Publishing Ltd.
51 Southgate Street, Winchester, Hants. SO23 9EH
www.ransom.co.uk

ISBN 978 184167 626 5
First published in 2007
Second printing 2008

A CIP catalogue record of this book is available from the British Library.

Design & layout: *www.macwiz.co.uk*
Printed in China through Colorcraft Ltd., Hong Kong.

Find out more about Boffin Boy at *www.ransom.co.uk*.

BOFFIN BOY AND THE ICE CAVES OF PLUTO

By David Orme
Illustrated by Peter Richardson

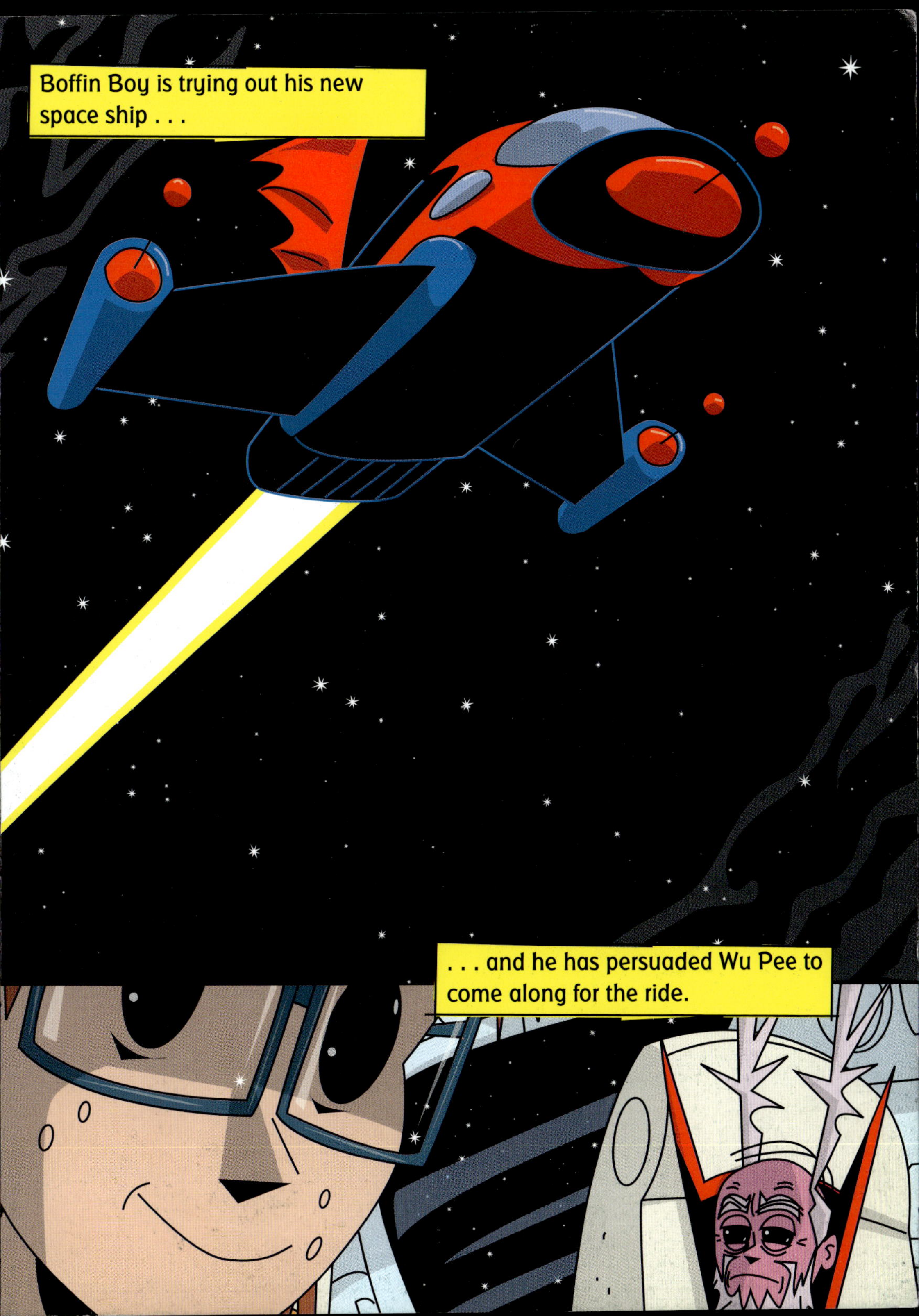

Boffin Boy is trying out his new space ship . . .

. . . and he has persuaded Wu Pee to come along for the ride.

But why does it have to be Pluto? It isn't even a planet any more.

I've just got this feeling that there is something amazing there.

That's Pluto, Wu Pee!
And that's its moon,
Charon, over there.

Welcome to Pluto, Wu Pee!
Thanks, Boffin Boy.
Can we go home now?

Boffin Boy wanted to explore, but Wu Pee had forgotten to put on his woolly space socks . . .

It's one small step for a superhero . . .

Oh, for goodness' sake shut up, Boffin Boy. My feet are freezing!

There's something strange under this hill.
Well, it will have to stay there. I'm not digging through that lot.

No need. We can explore this cave. Don't worry, Wu Pee, it will be perfectly safe.

Where have I heard that before?

I hope we're not going to get lost in here.

No problem, Wu Pee, I remember the way out.

So which way is it then?
This way! Er, no, that way . . . Just don't worry about it, Wu Pee.

An alien space ship, frozen in the ice! It could have been here for millions of years!

We're going to be here for millions of years too, if we can't find the way out of these caves.

Luckily, I have brought along my twiddly thing that will open any door . . .

Any minute now he's going to say 'Hey presto!' That really winds me up.

Hey presto!

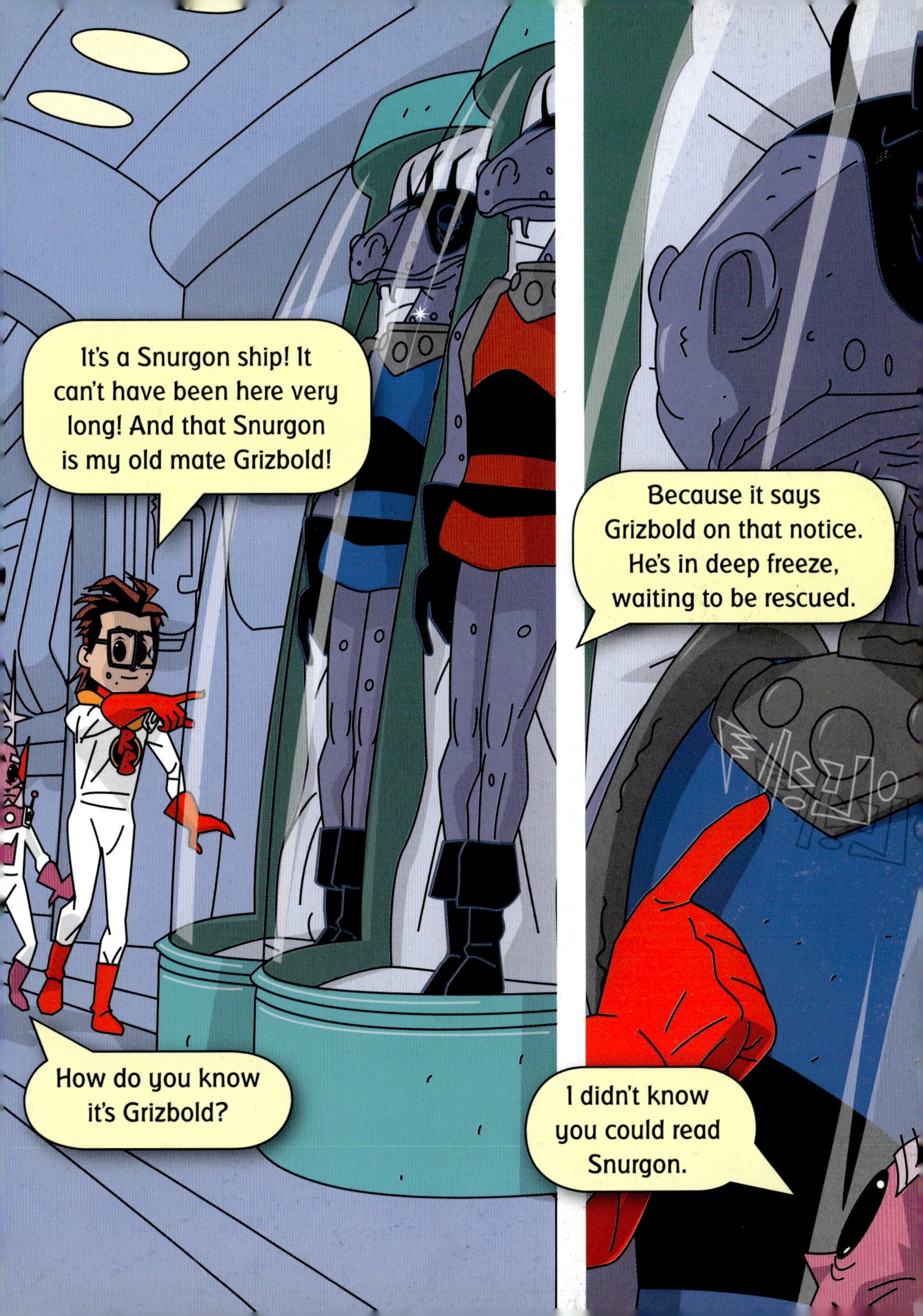

It's a Snurgon ship! It can't have been here very long! And that Snurgon is my old mate Grizbold!
How do you know it's Grizbold?
Because it says Grizbold on that notice. He's in deep freeze, waiting to be rescued.
I didn't know you could read Snurgon.

There's lots about me you don't know, Wu Pee. Now I'm about to wake them up, so go and put the kettle on.

So what happened, Grizbold?
You remember how short of water our planet is, Boffin Boy? There's lots of ice here on Pluto, so I was sent to get some.

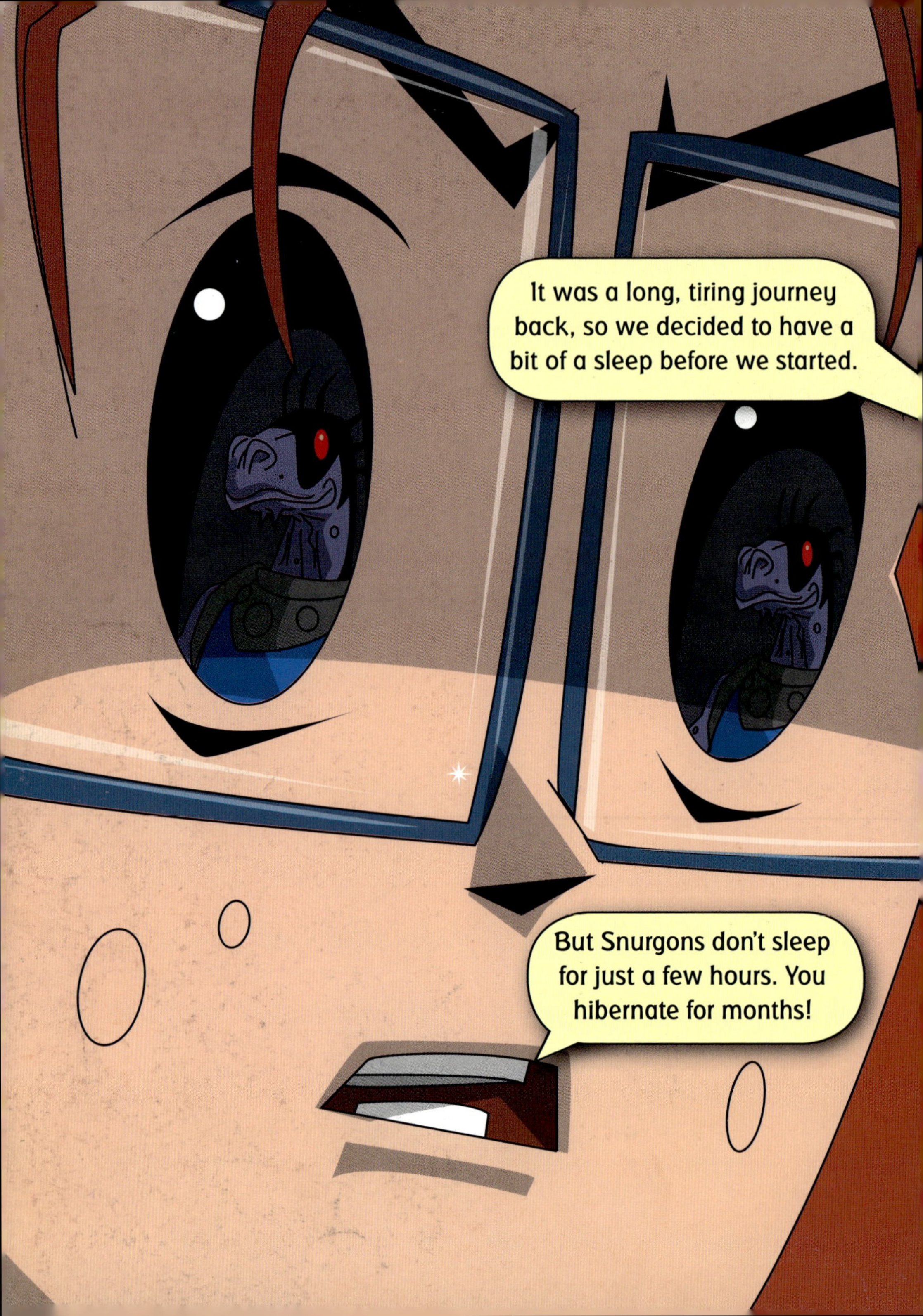

It was a long, tiring journey back, so we decided to have a bit of a sleep before we started.

But Snurgons don't sleep for just a few hours. You hibernate for months!

I told you we were tired.
Anyway, while we were
asleep it started to snow . . .

When we woke up, the ship was covered in snow and we couldn't move! So we thought we might as well go back to sleep again.

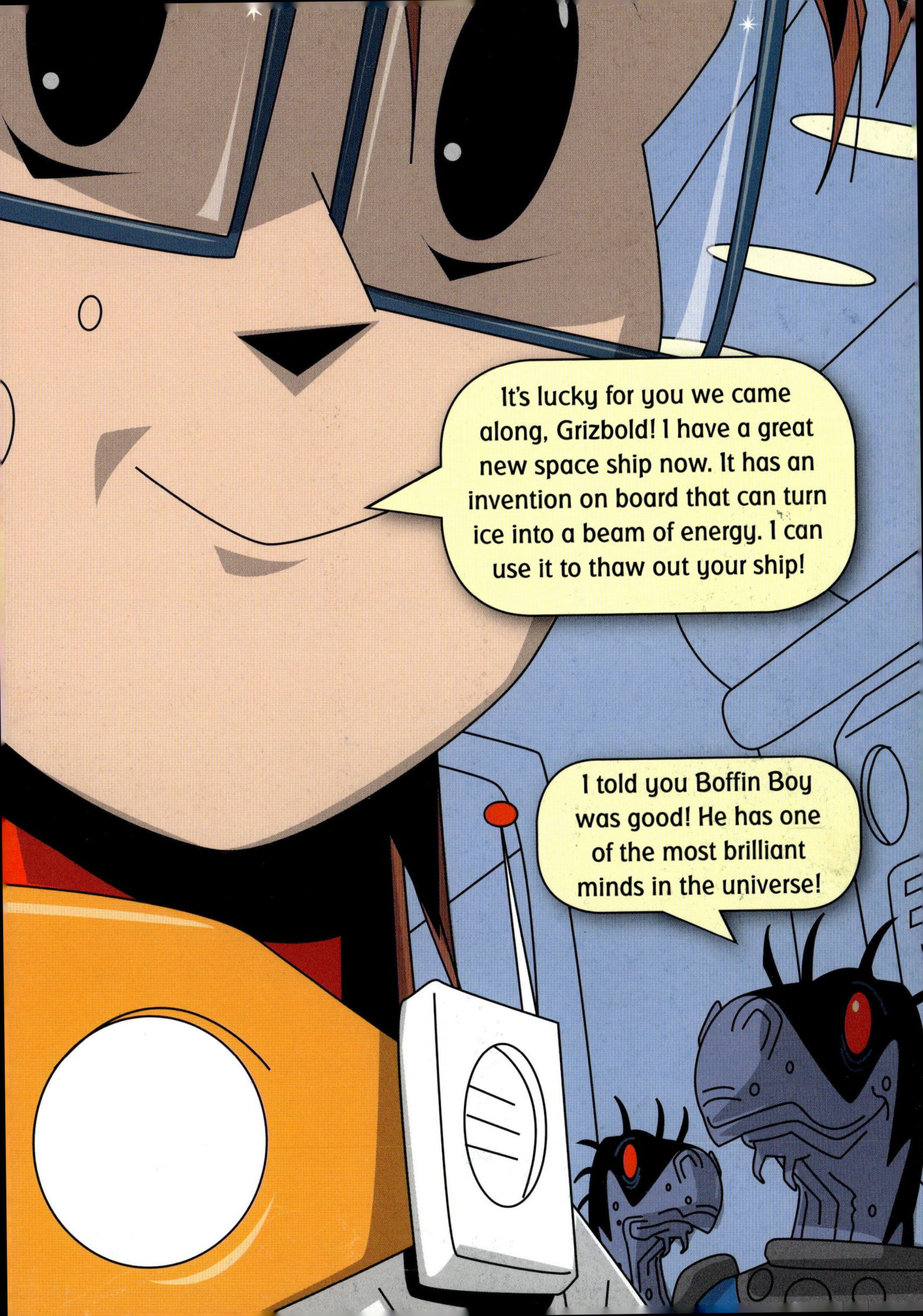

It's lucky for you we came along, Grizbold! I have a great new space ship now. It has an invention on board that can turn ice into a beam of energy. I can use it to thaw out your ship!

I told you Boffin Boy was good! He has one of the most brilliant minds in the universe!

So you're telling me you don't know the way out of these caves?

I'll get us out of here. Just trust me, Grizbold.

I wouldn't if I were you.

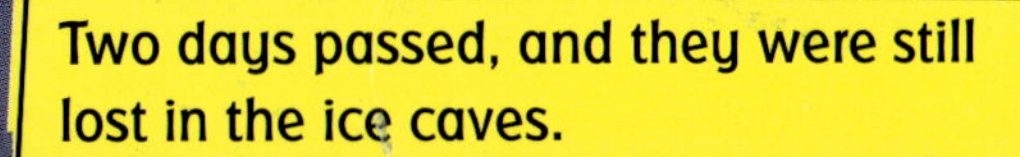
Two days passed, and they were still lost in the ice caves.
What was that you were saying about this fella's brilliant brain?

At last, they found the cave entrance.

The gang are in for a shock . . .
Oh no!

It's been snowing again . . .

Don't worry, Boffin Boy
can use his invention
to melt the ice!
Hmm. Exactly where is
this invention, Boffin Boy?
Er – it's in the
space ship.
BB

I'll never see my home planet again!

And my feet will never be warm again! It's no good, I'll have to try something!

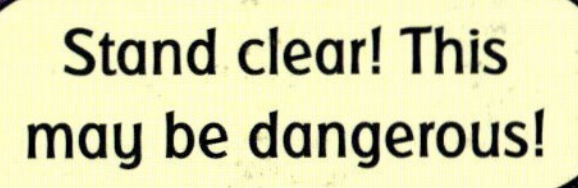
Stand clear! This may be dangerous!

Wu Pee, that was brilliant! Where did you learn to do that?

I saw someone do it in a movie. I've been meaning to give it a go.

And so the two ships get ready to take off from Pluto . . .

Come on, Wu Pee. It's take-off time!

No thanks. I'm getting a lift from Grizbold. He knows the way to Earth – and he's going to take a short cut!

ABOUT THE AUTHOR

David Orme has written over 200 books including poetry collections, fiction and non-fiction, and school text books. When he is not writing books he travels around the UK, giving performances, running writing workshops and courses.

Find out more at:
www.magic-nation.com.